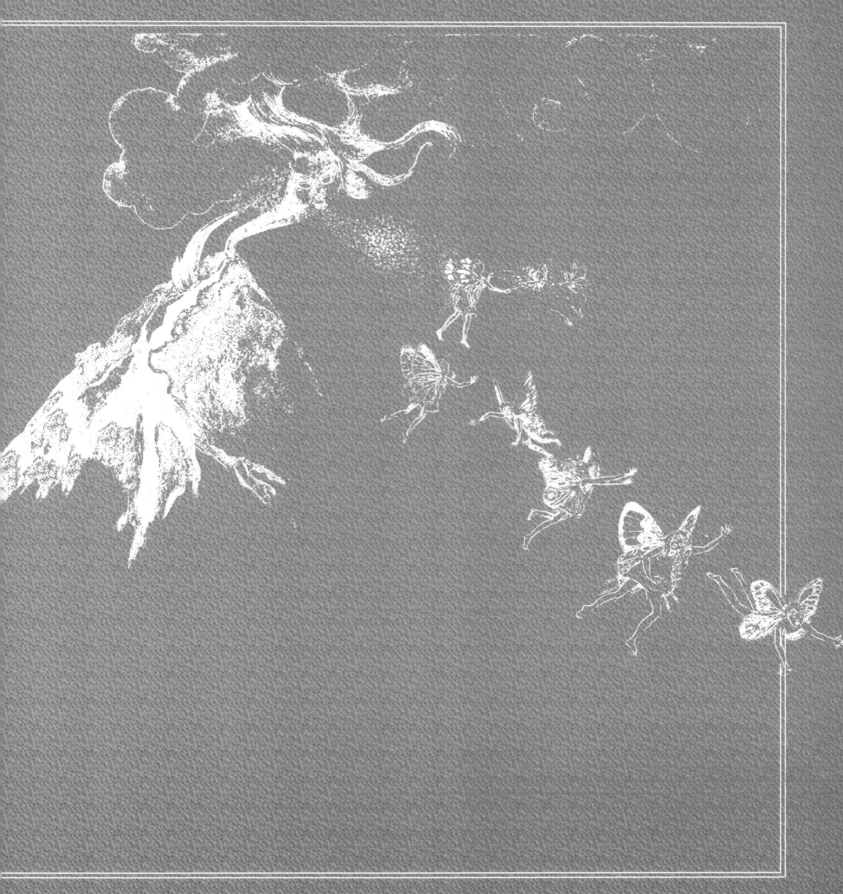

The Stowaway Fairy
A Hawaii Volcano Adventure
Written and Illustrated by Mary Koski

Island Heritage Publishing
Copyright © 1995
First Edition, Third Printing - 1999

Address orders and correspondence to:

ISLAND HERITAGE
P U B L I S H I N G
99-880 IWAENA STREET
HONOLULU, HAWAII 96701- 3202
(808) 487-7299

The Stowaway Fairy

A Hawaii Volcano Adventure

By Mary Koski

Rosie, the garden fairy, woke with a start as the suitcase she was traveling in was tossed onto a bed.

"Home at last," she thought happily.

She had had a wonderful adventure in Hawaii and she could hardly wait to tell the other Vermont garden fairies all about it.
As the suitcase was opened, Rosie was up and away with a whirr of her tiny wings.
But -- she stopped in mid-flight and hung in the air looking around. This was not the room she had expected to see.

"Where in the world am I now?" she thought.

She fluttered to the window and looked out. It was misty and a soft rain was falling.
No, it wasn't Vermont and it certainly wasn't Waikiki. All at once the clouds parted and Rosie was looking at the most enormous hole in the ground she had ever seen.

Just then she heard her couple from Vermont talking.

"I'm sure glad we found out about the blizzard back home and managed to get our tickets changed at the last minute like that!" said the man. "Besides, I'm really looking forward to exploring the Hawaii Volcanoes National Park. Imagine being practically on top of an active volcano!"

"Well, I wasn't ready to go home anyway," laughed the lady, "and five more days of vocation sounds good to me!"

"Five more days!" thought Rosie, "What fun!"

She couldn't wait to get out of the room. She wondered if there were any gardens here. She had no idea what a volcano was, but felt sure that she could find another fairy to ask.

Rosie could see that there was no balcony and that there was little chance of getting out by the window, so she watched carefully... and when the lady picked up her purse, she flew over and clung to the strap as the couple left the room.

When they turned toward the hotel dining room, Rosie let go and looked for an opening that led outside. She flew through a huge room where a fire crackled in a big fireplace and then she was out into the cool, moist evening.

There wasn't really a garden, but everywhere she looked were flowering trees, tiny orchids and large leafed plants topped by elegant red and yellow flowers. Everything was wet and shiny and dripping. Rosie alit on a broad leaf and instantly lost her footing. Down she slid, and off its tip she fell, landing with a splash in a tiny puddle of water.

Every leaf near her

was moving, and she thought she
heard giggling. Suddenly she was
surrounded by fairies, looking down at her
and laughing merrily.

These fairies were not at all like the fairies at the hotel
Rosie had just left in Waikiki. They were taller and darker
and dressed very differently. But they looked friendly,
so Rosie smiled a watery little smile.

A handsome boy fairy stepped forward and, reaching down, helped Rosie to her feet. Two others dried her off with soft golden fibers from some large ferns growing nearby.

"Aloha! This is Maili and this, Lehua," said the boy fairy, pointing to the two fairies who had dried her. "I am called Ohia. We are the fairies of the forest."

"Oh," said Rosie,

"That's why you look a little different. I'm a garden fairy, and I've been visiting some garden fairies in Waikiki." At this the forest fairies looked at Rosie with interest.

"Did you happen to meet a tall boy fairy with splendid red wings?" asked Lehua.

"Do you mean Koa?" cried Rosie.

"Oh yes!" chorused the others, crowding around and all beginning to ask questions at once.

Finally, Ohia, who seemed to be their leader, hushed them and told Rosie, "Koa is our cousin. He is really one of us, named for the tallest, most wonderful tree in the forest. He is visiting Honolulu and we all miss him. You must fly with us to our forest and meet the rest of his ohana."

At Rosie's puzzled look, he explained that "ohana" means family in Hawaiian, and family is very important to all Hawaiians - even Hawaiian fairies.

"I guess I belong to an 'ohana' too, back in Vermont," said Rosie a little wistfully.

"Come!" said Ohia. "It will be dark soon and we should be safely inside by then." Taking Rosie's hands, he and his twin Lehua flew up into the misty sunset sky, and all the fairies followed.

They flew near the vast black hole in the ground that Rosie had seen from the window. "That is the Halemaumau fire pit, home of Madam Pele, the fire goddess," said Lehua. "She can be fierce!" she added.

"Shouldn't we be afraid then?" whispered Rosie, eyeing the pit nervously.

"Never fear," laughed Ohia, "we are so small and insignificant that I'm sure the mighty Pele doesn't even know that we exist."

"Well, that's a relief," sighed Rosie, "but are there any other creatures in this forest of yours that I should watch out for?"

"See those lights?" said Ohia, pointing to some yellow glows bobbing along the forest floor. "Those belong to the Menehunes and although they are smaller than humans, they are fierce and warlike. They can see us, so be careful and stay out of their way."

"There are also animals in the forest, and the most fearsome is the mongoose," put in Maili. "He has sharp teeth and could snap your wings right off."

"Goodness! I'm not sure I want to go into your forest," said Rosie, "It sounds like a dangerous place, not at all like a garden. All we have to worry about in a garden is an occasional cat!"

"Oh, we have those too ~ wild ones," piped up Lehua.

"Great!" thought Rosie as the troupe of fairies drifted down through the trees to land in front of a cozy tree-stump cottage.

There they were greeted by more fairies who looked curiously at Rosie. When they heard she was a friend of Koa's, they escorted her inside, laughing and chattering.

That evening, they ate berries and wild mushrooms and many other things Rosie had never eaten before. They exchanged adventures and the Hawaiian fairies laughed and said they were "talking story." There was music and singing and now and then someone got up to dance. Rosie had a wonderful time!

It was late when they curled up to sleep. No one noticed the eyes peering through the window, or saw the golden light from the lantern bobbing away in the darkness.

Rosie shared a mossy bed with little Liko, and as she drifted to sleep, she thought how much more exciting it was in Hawaii than in her garden in Vermont.

She awoke to a strong jolt. In fact, she and Liko were bounced right out of bed! All around them fairies were crying out in alarm. Rosie could see their mouths moving, but there was such a loud roaring coming from everywhere that she couldn't hear their voices. She tried to stand up but was tossed into the air by a violent shudder of the ground.

Real terror was building in her stomach and reaching up into her chest. She thought her little heart would burst with fear! And then Ohia was beside her crying in her ear.

"Fly up, Rosie! It will be over soon!" Rosie noticed that all of the other fairies had taken to the air. Even little Liko was hovering above her.

"What is it?" She yelled at Ohia.

"It's an earthquake - Madam Pele is waking up!" Ohia yelled back.

"Don't be afraid. It won't last long."

Any time at all was too long for Rosie. From the air she could see the ground moving. Then, as suddenly as it began, it quit. The world was still again and silent. One after another, birds in the trees began to twitter. The fairies were calling to one another.

"Is everyone all right?"

One fairy had been bumped on the head by a falling bowl. Some things in the cottages had fallen down, but nothing was broken.

Long after it was all over, Rosie was still shaking. She could hardly believe it had only lasted a few seconds. She sat on a little rock almost wishing she was back home in Vermont.

Maili and Ohia flew down and sat beside her.

"You are in luck, Rosie!" said Maili smiling. "Sometimes an earthquake means that the volcano is going to erupt! You must see it while you are here. It's fun! You shouldn't miss it!"

"Oh, no!" said Rosie, rolling her eyes. "Last time someone said <u>that</u> to me I got into all sorts of trouble!"

She was remembering when Koa had taken her to see the ocean.

"This is different," Ohia urged her, "We don't dare go close. If we singed our wings, that would be the end of us!"

Rosie shuddered. It would be much worse than getting them wet, and that had been bad enough! She hoped Pele still slept.

However, when night fell, there was an orange glow in the sky.

Rosie hoped no one would notice, but soon everyone was making plans to fly to see the strange and wonderful sight.

Ohia took Rosie's hand. "I won't let anything happen to you," he said seriously. Looking into his eyes, Rosie knew she would be safe with him. So, without another word, they followed the other fairies over the tree tops and set off to find the source of the red glow.

They flew for a long time until suddenly there was a shout from the fairies up ahead and Rosie caught her breath. There before them was a towering fountain of blazing red lava. It leapt into the air and billows of smoke rose from it. All around, there was a fearsome roar.

Putting his mouth close to Rosie's ear, Ohia said, "Look carefully into the smoke and tell me what you see."

Rosie looked hard at the billowing smoke. It was just smoke - or was it? She looked again and almost cried out in amazement. There was a shape in the smoke and she could clearly see the uplifted arms, the flowing hair and the beautiful, terrifying face of the fire goddess Pele.

"Oh, Ohia, are you sure she can't see us?" gasped Rosie.
"I imagine she can see us," said Ohia, "but she doesn't seem to care
about us." He smiled reassuringly at Rosie, but in the red light
even <u>his</u> face looked frightening.

Just then the figure in the smoke seemed to turn and look directly at the little group of
fairies. Leaning forward, she blew a bright bubble of lava from her mouth right toward
them! They could all feel the heat as the glowing ball flew lazily through the air. Then
they were in frantic flight back toward their forest. The ball was left behind, but all the
way back to the kipuka* they could hear Pele's amused chuckle.

"Well, I guess she has noticed us," panted Ohia as they landed in the cool grass.

"Do you think she meant to hurt us?" asked Rosie, half expecting to see the goddess
coming after them.

*Kipuka— opening in the forest or oasis in lava bed.

It was everyone's opinion that Pele had just been playing with them, because, as Maili pointed out, if she had wanted to hurt them, she certainly could have. After that, it was agreed that they had all had more than enough excitement for one day, so the weary fairies folded their wings and went to sleep.

During the next few days,

Rosie's new friends introduced her to their forest. It was very different from the gardens she had seen, but wonderful in its own way. There were long vines of fragrant maile. Interesting trees called ohia were everywhere, their leaves green and grey and pink, with bursts of scarlet flowers on the tips of their branches. There was the tall koa tree that her friend was named for. Ferns covered the forest floor, from ones so tall she couldn't see their tops, to tiny ones, growing out of the velvety moss.

The Hawaiian fairies showed Rosie how they gathered materials for their tiny leis - always thanking the plant... and never taking more than they needed.

"You must treat the 'aina' - the land - with respect," Ohia told Rosie seriously. "A forest is like a garden in many ways. Tend it carefully, and it will reward you with many wonders."

Rosie loved the way her Hawaiian friend talked. "How special you forest fairies are and how wonderful your forest! I will never forget this visit and what you have taught me." She would have loved to hug Ohia right then, but she was too shy.

21

All day the fairies worked and played among the trees, but when evening came on Rosie's last day, delicious smells from the little moss - covered cottages made them turn toward home.

"It's luau time," called Liko, the littlest fairy, flying out to meet them with arms outstretched. "I must call everyone to the party!" and she flitted by, her tiny wings flapping madly.

It was a wonderful party. Fairies came from all parts of the forest. There was more food than Rosie had ever seen in one place before and it was laid out in a beautiful way on ferns and shiny leaves.
Speeches of greeting were made. Songs were sung and dances were danced.

Rosie was having more fun than she could ever remember having before until someone stood up, and looking carefully around the room asked, "Has anyone seen little Liko?"

It was suddenly very quiet as all the fairies looked at one another for an answer and then looked around the room. The party forgotten, they rushed to the door, remembering that the last time Liko had been seen, she was flying out to call fairies to the luau.

Ohia and Lehua made up search parties which flew out into the dark forest.

"Stay inside since you don't know the forest," said Ohia to Rosie as he lit a little lantern and started out the door. "We don't want you to get lost, too," he called back over his shoulder.

Rosie stood at the door. How she wished she could help, but she knew Ohia was right. She could hear the fairies calling in the distance. Then they were too far away to hear and Rosie felt very lonely indeed.

It seemed such a long time that she stood in the doorway watching and listening, but the forest stayed dark and quiet. Then - there was a little sound. Was it a call for help? Rosie turned her head this way and that. There it was again! It <u>was</u> a cry for help! It was very, very faint, but clearly a voice.

Rosie lit two lanterns. One she turned up as high as she could and put it in the doorway to lead her back to the cottage, and the other she held before her as she flew off into the darkness.

Not far from the cottage the sound became louder. Sure enough, in a shaft of moonlight sat Liko, rubbing her eyes and crying and calling for help between her sobs.

Rosie landed in front of her, and kneeling down, held out her arms to the tiny fairy. Liko threw herself into them and hugged Rosie with all her might.

"Oh, I'm so glad you've come for me! I've been out here in the dark <u>forever</u>!" she cried dramatically.

"Come, come," soothed Rosie. "You're all right now. Let's fly home and surprise everyone when they get back."

Just then there was a rustle from under a nearby bush and bright red eyes glowed in the light from Rosie's lantern. A sleek head appeared, followed by a long slinky body. Rosie's hair stood straight up.
Ordinarily the mongoose didn't hunt at night, but a snack of two little fairies was too good to pass up.

"Oh," cried Liko, "Bad mongoose! Let's go, Rosie!" Rosie hugged Liko to her and shot up into the air, but she failed to notice the dry branches and twigs right above her. One flap of her wings and she was caught. She and Liko dangled above the mongoose's nose.

The mongoose sniffed at Rosie's little foot and licked its lips. It opened its mouth to take a bite, but Rosie pulled her feet up as far as she could.

The mongoose stood on its hind legs and opened its mouth wide! How many teeth it had! Rosie screamed and closed her eyes...and...

Nothing happened. Rosie opened her eyes. The mongoose was no longer interested in her, but in a sturdy figure who carried a lantern in one hand and a long heavy spear in the other. He carefully set the lantern down, and then, with lightning speed, he hit the mongoose a stunning blow on its tender nose.

The animal fled, helped on its way by another blow, this time to its tail. Then the menehune (Rosie knew at once what he was) turned his attention to the two fairies.

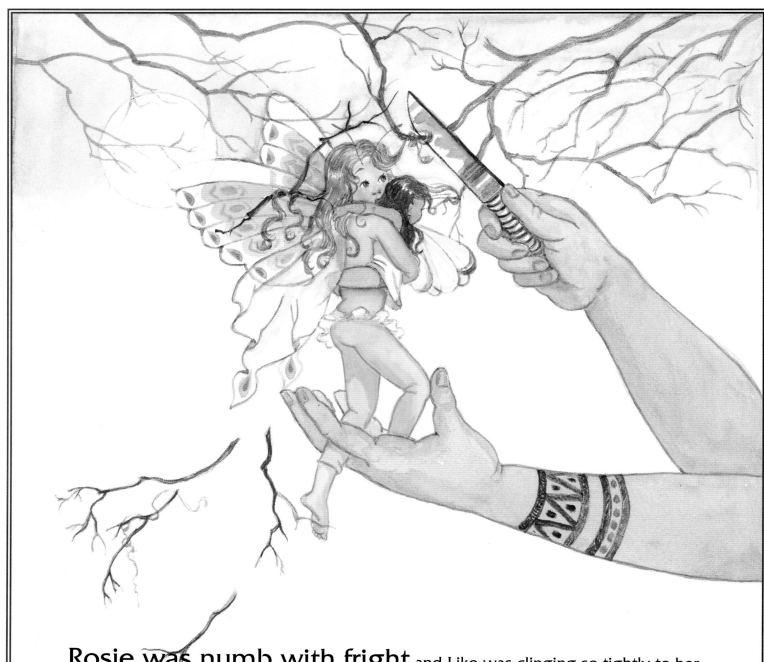

Rosie was numb with fright and Liko was clinging so tightly to her that she could hardly breathe.

"Auwe*, poor little fairies. You really got yourselves in trouble, didn't you?"

The young menehune took a sharp knife out of his belt and carefully cut the twigs holding Rosie's wings. He caught the two fairies as they fell and placed them gently on the ground.

"There you are. Run along home now," he smiled.

*Auwe — Used to express wonder, fear, scorn, pity, affection.

"Wait a minute," said Rosie, as she pried Liko's arms from around her neck and stood her on the ground.

"You can't save us and then just send us home like - like we were babies!"

"Why not?" asked the menehune, squatting down in front of this curiously brave fairy.

"Because I want to thank you, and, well, I want to get to know you. You seem really nice and I can't imagine why the forest fairies fear you so much. Are all menehune like you?" demanded Rosie.

The menehune looked at Rosie in amazement. He had no idea that fairies talked so much. "Yes," he replied. "Are all fairies like you?"

"Of course," said Rosie. "You're a bit bigger than we are, but I'll bet we're a lot alike. I even know a human child, and she's just the same too, only bigger yet."

The menehune was impressed. "My name is Kalopa," he offered. "What are you called?"

"Oh, I'm Tea Rose, but you can call me Rosie," smiled the fairy. "This little fairy is Liko."

"Good name," he laughed, "little bud."

"Come home with us now and meet the ohana. I think it's time you all got to know one another," said Rosie, tugging at his hand.

When the unsuccessful searchers

sadly returned to the cottage, they were amazed to find Rosie and Liko sitting in the yard sipping ohelo-berry tea with a menehune.

They fell back in terror until Rosie smiled and called to them, and Liko climbed up on the menehune's knee to show them that they had nothing to fear.

Rosie took Ohia and Lehua by the hands and led them to her large friend.

"All these years," she said, "you thought the menehune meant you harm and they thought you silly and flighty and not worth their interest. When will creatures ever learn to get to know one another?"

Kalopa smiled and offered a finger to Ohia to shake. Without hesitation, Ohia took it in his firm little fairy hand.

"Are all menehune like you?" he asked.

"Yes," laughed Kalopa, "and I hear that you fairies are not at all what we thought you to be."

"Just think what good things we could accomplish in the forest working together!" said Lehua. "You must invite your friends and family to a big meeting! We will gather all the forest fairies and we will have a big makahiki! There will be song and dance and food..."

"And games," put in Kalopa excitedly. "I will tell all the menehune and we will bring food and mats and..."

Lehua and Kalopa

were soon happily making plans for the big gathering.
But Rosie said sadly to Ohia, "I'm so sorry that I won't be able to stay for the party.
This morning I must return to the hotel so that I can get back in my suitcase and go
back to Vermont."

"Stay, Rosie," begged Ohia, "You seem one of us already."

For a second Rosie was tempted. The forest was so beautiful and the Hawaiian
fairies so warm and loving, but...

"No," she said. "My family would worry and I would miss them.
I must go home, but maybe someday I can come back to visit."

Although none of the fairies wanted her to go,
they all understood. Ohia and Maili
and Lehua flew back to the
Volcano House with Rosie
to see her off.

As they reached the hotel, Rosie saw two familiar figures getting into a taxi. It was her Vermont couple! Her suitcase was put into the trunk, and with a roar, they were off. Rosie and her friends flew as fast as they could, but soon the car was only a speck on the road in front of them.

"Oh, no," cried Rosie. "Now I'll never get home!" And she began to sob.

"Don't cry, Rosie," said Ohia, "Maybe we can catch up with them at the airport. It's too far to fly ourselves, but we have a route that all the island fairies use. Come along."

The fairies flew to a greenhouse where orchids were grown for leis.

"Look!" said Maili, pointing, "There is a delivery truck just ready to leave for the Hilo airport. Quick, Rosie! Into one of the boxes!"

They sped to the truck, raised the corner of a flower box lid and slipped inside. It was dark, but the flowers made a soft bed and the fairies settled down for their trip.

FRAGILE

FLOWER

The Lei Maker
Honolulu, H.

Will pick up

Ph: 808-935-7729

When the flowers were unloaded at the airport, the fairies cautiously climbed out of their box. They saw a line of people waiting with their suitcases at the agricultural inspection station. Rosie was delighted to see her Vermont family standing in the line. And there was her suitcase! But, it was shut tight.

"You have one more chance, Rosie," said Ohia. "When your suitcase is opened for inspection, you must be inside before it is closed again. Sometimes it goes fast, so you won't have much time."

Her people were nearly at the head of the line, so Rosie quickly hugged her friends who had become so much like a family to her in such a short time.

"Don't forget me," she whispered.

"How could we ever forget you, Rosie," smiled Ohia. Lehua and Maile nodded, their eyes bright with tears.

Then Rosie's family was at the head of the line. Her suitcase was lifted onto the counter. The big inspector was opening it.

"Now!" cried the fairies, and Rosie shot forward and practically tumbled into her suitcase.

"Hey, Mommy!" cried a little boy whose family was next in line. "A fairy just flew into that suitcase!"

"Not now, Kris," said his mother, who was busy counting suitcases.

"Look, Mommy! I'll show you," he cried, dashing forward and making a grab for Rosie who was frantically trying to bury herself in the clothes.

"Hey! Careful, Buddy," said the inspector, "You don't want to get your fingers pinched!" And with that, he snapped the suitcase shut and slapped a green sticker across the lock.

"But there's a fairy…," began the boy.

"Move along - **next**!" said the inspector, and Rosie was on her way home.

U.S. DEPARTMENT OF
AGRICULTURE INSPECTION
Please declare all agricultural
items: (Fruit, plants, seeds, etc.)
WARNING:
A civil penalty may be assessed
if undeclared agricultural items
are found.

Section 10 of the plant quarantine
act:

38

As Rosie's couple settled

themselves in their seats, the man said to his wife, "Don't laugh, but I heard that darn hummingbird again."

She did laugh.

The fairies watched the plane as it lifted into the sky. They knew their lives would never be the same without Rosie's bright presence. They all hoped she would return some day - especially Ohia.

In her suitcase, Rosie snuggled down to sleep away the long hours until she would be home again. But when she dreamed, it was not of Vermont. Her dreams were filled with the scent of ginger blossoms and visions of the cool green kipuka and her new ohana at the Volcano.

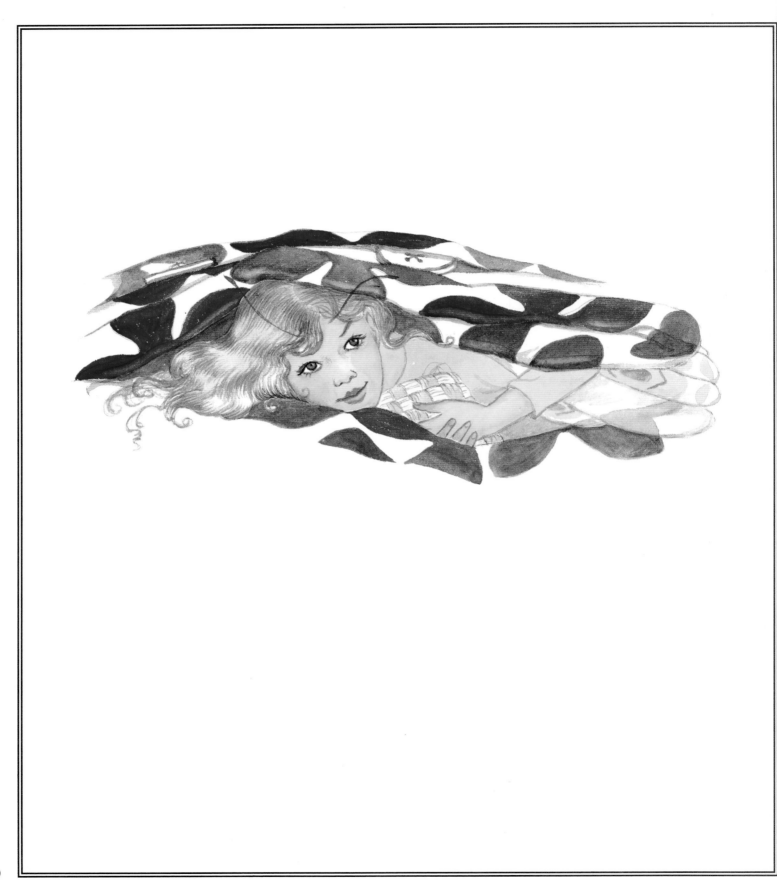